Y0-BVR-682

THE BEAGLE
HAS LANDED

© 1958, 1965 United Feature Syndicate, Inc.

Peanuts Parade Paperbacks

THE BEAGLE HAS LANDED

© 1952, 1958, 1965 United Feature Syndicate, Inc.

by Charles M. Schulz

Holt, Rinehart and Winston / New York

PEANUTS comic strips by Charles M. Schulz

Copyright © 1977, 1978 by United Feature Syndicate, Inc.

All rights reserved, including the right to reproduce this book or portions thereof in any form.

Published simultaneously in Canada by Holt, Rinehart and Winston of Canada, Limited.

First published in book form in 1978.

Library of Congress Catalog Card Number: 78-53776

ISBN: 0-03-044781-X

First Edition

Printed in the United States of America

10   9   8   7   6   5   4   3   2

© 1966 United Feature Syndicate, Inc.

PEANUTS comic strips to follow: © 1977 United Feature Syndicate, Inc.

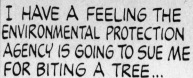

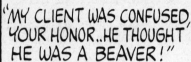

NOW THAT YOUR MASTER HAS RUN AWAY, I'M SUPPOSED TO FEED YOU

SOUNDS OMINOUS, DOESN'T IT?

I KNOW IT'S WRONG TO RUN AWAY...

BUT WHO WANTS TO GO TO JAIL? BESIDES BITING ONE TREE ISN'T GOING TO DESTROY THE ENVIRONMENT...

NO ONE'S GOING TO MISS ME ANYWAY... I NEVER DO ANYTHING RIGHT...

IF LIFE WERE A CAMERA, I'D HAVE THE LENS CAP ON

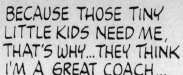

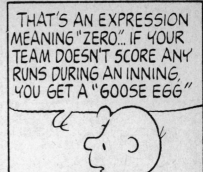

WHAT IN THE WORLD IS THAT?

IT'S A LIFE-SIZE POSTER OF MYSELF

I HAD IT MADE FROM A SMALL SNAPSHOT...I'M GOING TO GIVE IT TO MY MOM AND DAD AS A SURPRISE...

THAT'S A GREAT IDEA..I'D LIKE TO DO SOMETHING LIKE THAT MYSELF

DON'T! IT'S TOO RISKY...

AFTER THE PARENTS GET A POSTER, THEY MIGHT DECIDE THEY DON'T NEED THE KID!

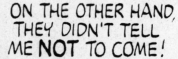

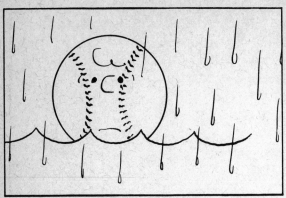

BANG
BANG
BANG

ALL RIGHT, WHO'S OUT THERE MAKING ALL THAT NOISE?

IT'S THE GARAGE

BANG
BANG
BANG
BANG

HE KEEPS HITTING 'EM BACK!

HITTING BALLS AGAINST THE GARAGE MUST BE GOOD PRACTICE...

IT'S PROBABLY ALSO FUN, ISN'T IT?

UNTIL SOMEONE PARKS THE CAR!

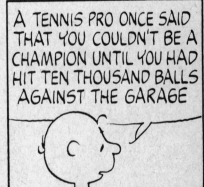

YOU KNOW WHERE CHAMPIONS ARE MADE?

WELL, THEY'RE NOT MADE AT WIMBLEDON OR FOREST HILLS, I'LL TELL YOU THAT!

THEY'RE MADE RIGHT HERE ON THESE DIRTY, BUMPY, MISERABLE COURTS WHERE YOU CALL YOUR OWN LINES AND KEEP YOUR OWN SCORE!

YOU GET WHAT YOU GO FOR, KID!

I'D LIKE TO GO HOME, BUT I THINK SHE'D KILL ME!

SEE THAT FAT LADY OVER THERE?

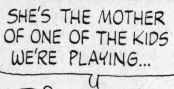

SHE'S THE MOTHER OF ONE OF THE KIDS WE'RE PLAYING...

SHE COMES TO SEE THAT HER LITTLE DARLING GETS GOOD CALLS! SHE HATES ME

SHE KNOWS THAT WHEN I'M PLAYING, ALL THE CALLS ARE GOING TO BE IN CENTIMETERS!

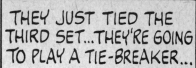

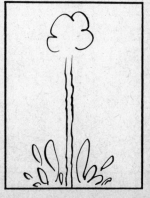

I'M GOING TO BE A CADDY, MARCIE

THIS IS A JOB APPLICATION FOR THE COUNTRY CLUB

CAN YOU CARRY A BAG OF GOLF CLUBS, SIR?

CARRY?! I THOUGHT A CADDY JUST DROVE THE GOLF CART...

COME ON ALONG, MARCIE

WE'LL GO OVER TO THE COUNTRY CLUB, AND GET JOBS AS CADDIES.. WE'LL MAKE A FORTUNE

I CAN'T TELL A PAR FROM A BIRDIE, SIR...

THOSE ARE BOWLING TERMS, MARCIE..DON'T EMBARRASS ME!

AAUGH!

WHAT ARE YOU DOING IN THAT SAND TRAP, MARCIE?

I THINK SOMEBODY LEFT THE DOOR OPEN..

SIR?

WHY ARE THE TWO LADIES SCREAMING AT EACH OTHER?

THEY'RE ARGUING ABOUT THE SCORE

PUSH HER IN THE LAKE, MA'AM!!

STAY OUT OF IT, MARCIE!

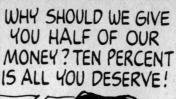

War and Punishment

Crime and Peace

"You didn't keep your promise," she said.

"When I married you, you said we'd live in a vine-covered cottage."

"All right! All right!" he shouted

"You go talk to the Planning Commission!"

※WHEW※ I DON'T KNOW WHAT'S WRONG WITH ME LATELY...

I WALK ABOUT ONE BLOCK, AND I GET SO WEAK I CAN HARDLY DRAG THIS BLANKET...

THERE'S NO EXCUSE FOR MISSING A BALL LIKE THAT! THERE'S ABSOLUTELY NO EXCUSE!

THE MOONS OF SATURN GOT IN MY EYES!

I TAKE IT BACK... THAT WASN'T A BAD EXCUSE...

I THOUGHT YOU WENT TO SUMMER CAMP...

HOW DID YOU GET OUT OF GOING?

I FOLLOWED A VERY SIMPLE PLAN...

I HID UNDER MY BED FOR THREE WEEKS!

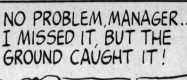

RATS! MY TOMATO PLANTS AREN'T DOING A THING!

I KNEW YOU WERE HAVING TROUBLE SO I CALLED IN THE CROP DUSTER

CROP DUSTER?!

WHAT CROP DUSTER?

CHOP CHOP CHOP CHOP

WHOOSH!!

CHOP CHOP CHOP

CHOP CHOP

OH.....THAT CROP DUSTER...

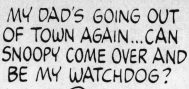

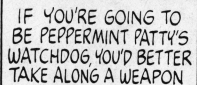

CHUCK, YOU GET OVER HERE RIGHT AWAY!

SNOOPY WAS YOUR RESPONSIBILITY! IF HE'S RUN OUT ON ME, YOU'RE GONNA TAKE HIS PLACE!

YOU'RE GONNA BE THE WATCHDOG, CHUCK! DO YOU HEAR ME?!

WOOF!

YOU SURE TOOK YOUR SWEET TIME GETTING OVER HERE, CHUCK

I COULD HAVE BEEN MUGGED TWENTY TIMES BY NOW! ANYWAY, SNOOPY LEFT SO YOU HAVE TO BE MY WATCHDOG...

I'LL BE YOUR WATCHDOG, AND I'LL SIT OUT HERE ON THE PORCH, BUT I WON'T WEAR **THAT**!

OKAY, CHUCK, WE'LL FORGET THE COLLAR

OKAY, WATCHDOG, YOU CAN WAKE UP.. IT'S MORNING!

WOW! THAT WAS A LONG NIGHT... I DON'T THINK I'D MAKE A GOOD WATCHDOG...

SNOOPY! WHERE HAVE YOU BEEN?

AROUND THE WORLD AND BACK! I'M IN LOVE!!

WEDDING INVITATIONS?

I'M GETTING MARRIED! I'VE MET THE MOST WONDERFUL GIRL IN THE WORLD!

ALL MY LIFE I'VE FELT UNSETTLED... SORT OF UP IN THE AIR...NOT ANY MORE..

THE BEAGLE HAS LANDED!

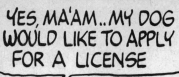

I'D SURE LIKE TO KNOW WHAT THIS FUTURE WIFE OF YOURS LOOKS LIKE

SHE HAS BEAUTIFUL BROWN EYES... A FANTASTIC SMILE...

AND A CUTE LITTLE NOSE JUST LIKE YOURS!

SMAK!!

THAT'S THE ONLY WAY TO HANDLE A QUESTION LIKE THAT!

YES, SIR, MY DOG IS GETTING MARRIED...HE NEEDS A COMPLETE WEDDING OUTFIT...

NO, SIR, WE DON'T HAVE AN ACCOUNT HERE

I'M SURE MY CREDIT IS GOOD

INFORM THE GENTLEMAN THAT I WAS A WORLD WAR I FLYING ACE!

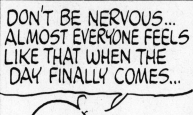

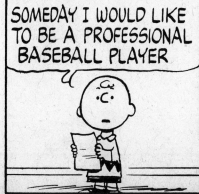

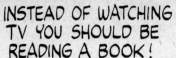

INSTEAD OF WATCHING TV YOU SHOULD BE READING A BOOK!

INSTEAD OF WATCHING TV YOU COULD BE STRAIGHTENING UP YOUR ROOM!

INSTEAD OF WATCHING TV YOU COULD EVEN BE PLAYING OUTSIDE!

THERE'S A LOT MORE TO LIFE THAN NOT WATCHING TV!

THIS IS THE TIME OF YEAR WHEN SOME OF THE LEAVES BEGIN TO FALL...

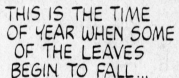

KLUNK

NOT THE BIRDS... JUST THE LEAVES!

JOGGING IS GOOD FOR THE SOUL AND THE BODY

WOODSTOCK KEEPS FALLING BEHIND

WHOOPS! THERE HE IS UP FRONT AGAIN...

NOW, HE'S BEHIND AGAIN..

I'LL BET HE DROPS BACK SO HE CAN FLY...

IT'S NOT FAIR TO FLY WHEN YOU'RE SUPPOSED TO BE JOGGING!

MAYBE I COULD LOOK AROUND REAL FAST, AND CATCH HIM...

ON THE OTHER HAND, I DON'T WANT HIM TO THINK I DON'T TRUST HIM...

ON THE OTHER HAND, I DON'T LIKE TO BE TAKEN ADVANTAGE OF, EITHER!

ON THE OTHER HAND..

WHO CARES?!

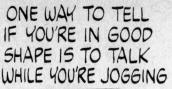

ONE WAY TO TELL IF YOU'RE IN GOOD SHAPE IS TO TALK WHILE YOU'RE JOGGING

IF YOU CAN CARRY ON A CONVERSATION WHILE YOU'RE JOGGING, THEN YOU'RE IN GOOD SHAPE

I'M SORRY I MENTIONED IT

SCHULZ

WOW! STAY OFF THE ROADS TODAY!

THIS IS NATIONAL JOGGING DAY...THERE MUST BE TEN BILLION JOGGERS OUT THERE!

IF YOU DON'T LOOK OUT, THEY'LL RUN RIGHT OVER YOU...

IS THAT WHAT HAPPENED?

SCHULZ

ARE YOU INTERESTED IN HAVING ME TELL YOU SOMETHING FOR YOUR OWN GOOD?

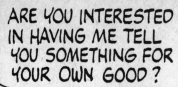

I'M NOT SURE

WELL, IF IT WILL HELP YOU TO MAKE UP YOUR MIND...

I'D ENJOY IT, TOO!

Joe Murmur and his brothers were pickpockets.

They worked all the county fairs.

How did people know their pockets were being picked?

When a Murmur ran through the crowd.

OKAY, THIS IS WHAT WE'LL DO...

YOU GO DOWN TO THE END OF THE FIELD, AND I'LL KICK THE BALL TO YOU

I'LL BE ALL ALONE DOWN THERE...

YOU WON'T BE ALONE..THE BALL WILL BE WITH YOU!

WHAT IF IT DOESN'T SHOW UP?

IT'LL BE THERE... I'M GOING TO KICK IT TO YOU

WHAT IF I GO ALL THE WAY DOWN THERE, AND I GET MUGGED?

HOW CAN YOU GET MUGGED? WE'RE THE ONLY ONES AROUND HERE!

THAT'S WHAT YOU SAY!

ANOTHER THING...SO I WALK ALL THE WAY DOWN THERE... HOW DO I KNOW YOU WON'T RUN OFF AND LEAVE ME?

OKAY, FORGET IT!

NO, THAT'S ALL RIGHT... I'LL DO IT

MY MOTHER WARNED ME THAT FOOTBALL WAS A RISKY GAME

THERE'S MORE TO FOOTBALL THAN JUST KICKING THE BALL

TODAY I'M GOING TO TEACH YOU HOW TO CATCH A FORWARD PASS...

ALL RIGHT, START RUNNING!

GET WAY OUT! WAY OUT!

BONK!

OKAY, NOW HERE'S WHAT YOU DID WRONG...

I KNOW WHAT I DID WRONG! I NEVER SHOULD HAVE SPOKEN TO YOU YEARS AGO! I NEVER SHOULD HAVE LET YOU INTO MY LIFE! I SHOULD HAVE WALKED AWAY! I SHOULD HAVE TOLD YOU TO GET LOST! THAT'S WHAT I DID WRONG, YOU BLOCKHEAD!!

YOU ALSO PROBABLY SHOULD HOLD YOUR HANDS A LITTLE CLOSER TOGETHER...

YOU KNOW WHAT?

I THINK I'VE LEARNED THE SECRET OF LIFE...

I WENT TO THE DOCTOR YESTERDAY BECAUSE I HAD A SORE THROAT...THE NURSE PUT ME IN A SMALL ROOM..

I COULD HEAR A KID IN ANOTHER ROOM SCREAMING HIS HEAD OFF...

WHEN THE DOCTOR CAME IN TO SEE ME, I TOLD HIM I WAS GLAD I WASN'T IN THAT OTHER ROOM ...

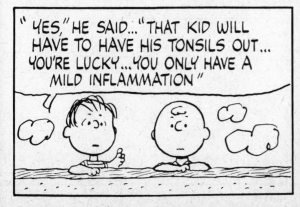

"YES," HE SAID..."THAT KID WILL HAVE TO HAVE HIS TONSILS OUT... YOU'RE LUCKY...YOU ONLY HAVE A MILD INFLAMMATION"

THE SECRET OF LIFE IS TO BE IN THE RIGHT ROOM !

HERE WE ARE...

NOW, THIS WILL BE SORT OF A REHEARSAL FOR TOMORROW NIGHT, SNOOPY...

TOMORROW IS HALLOWEEN, AND ON HALLOWEEN NIGHT THE GREAT PUMPKIN RISES OUT OF THE PUMPKIN PATCH, AND BRINGS TOYS TO ALL THE CHILDREN IN THE WORLD...

YOUR JOB IS TO BE KIND OF A PAUL REVERE...WHEN THE GREAT PUMPKIN COMES, YOU'LL GET ON YOUR HORSE, AND RIDE THROUGH THE COUNTRYSIDE SPREADING THE NEWS!

OKAY, LET'S REHEARSE IT..

HE'S COMING! HE'S COMING! THE GREAT PUMPKIN IS COMING!

RIDE, SNOOPY, RIDE! SPREAD THE NEWS!

I FEEL LIKE SUCH A FOOL!

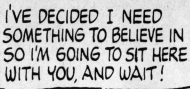

HAVE YOU EVER BEEN "DEPROGRAMMED," SIR?

IT'S TERRIBLE! MY FAMILY HAS BEEN YELLING AT ME ALL NIGHT...

APPARENTLY IT'S ALL RIGHT TO BELIEVE IN SANTA CLAUS, BUT IT'S WRONG TO BELIEVE IN THE "GREAT GRAPE"

I THINK THAT'S "PUMPKIN," MARCIE...

I'M STILL FEELING A LITTLE DIZZY.....

MY FAMILY SAID IT'S ALL RIGHT TO BELIEVE IN SANTA CLAUS, BUT NOT THE GREAT PUMPKIN

THEY SAID YOU WERE A FALSE PROPHET

WHAT ELSE?

THAT'S ALL.. NOTHING ELSE...

WHAT ELSE?

WELL, THEY ALSO SAID YOU WERE CRAZY..

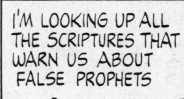

AH, WHAT A BEAUTIFUL DAY!

I THINK EVERYBODY ENJOYS TAKING A WALK THROUGH THE LEAVES ON A BRISK FALL DAY...

BONK!

WELL, ALMOST EVERYBODY

THE POLAR BEARS ARE IN TROUBLE TODAY

DIDN'T SEE ANY POLAR BEARS, HUH?

THAT'S A GOOD IDEA.. TRY THE OTHER DIRECTION...

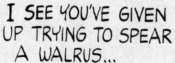

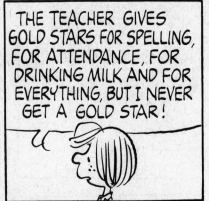

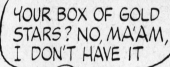

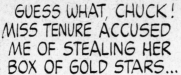

GUESS WHAT, CHUCK! MISS TENURE ACCUSED ME OF STEALING HER BOX OF GOLD STARS...

THAT'S HARD TO BELIEVE...

YOU'RE NOT KIDDING, CHUCK! IS MY STUPID ATTORNEY AROUND THERE ANY PLACE?

YES, HE'S RIGHT HERE...

"CURSE ON ALL LAWS BUT THOSE WHICH LOVE HAS MADE!"

I DIDN'T STEAL THAT BOX OF GOLD STARS, SNOOPY, BUT I'M GOING TO FIND OUT WHO DID...

NOW, HERE'S MY SECRET PLAN...

I LOVE SECRET PLANS

YOU'LL WEAR THIS WIG, SEE, AND YOU'LL SIT IN MY SEAT AT SCHOOL

?

WHILE YOU'RE DOING THAT, I'LL SNEAK AROUND AND FIND OUT WHO TOOK THE GOLD STARS!

SIR, WHAT ARE YOU DOING OUT HERE IN THE HALLWAY?

QUIET, MARCIE

I'M IN DISGUISE! I'M TRYING TO FIND OUT WHO TOOK THE BOX OF GOLD STARS...

BUT I JUST SAW YOU SITTING AT YOUR DESK...

THAT'S MY ATTORNEY... HE'S ALSO IN DISGUISE...

"I BEFORE E EXCEPT AFTER C"

YES, MA'AM..I'M HANS HANSEN, THE NEW CUSTODIAN...

JUST GO ON WITH YOUR TEACHING, MA'AM..I'LL SWEEP UP A BIT AND EMPTY THE WASTEBASKETS...

OH, I'M DREAMING OF MY SWEETHEART IN MINNEAPOLIS AND MY MOTHER IN ST. PAUL!

SORRY, MA'AM..I CAN'T HELP SINGING WHILE I SWEEP...

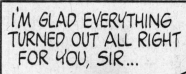

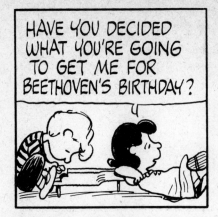

CLOMP CLOMP
CLOMP CLOMP

I KNEW I HEARD SOMEONE WALKING ON MY SANDWICH!

I SEE YOU ATE ALL OF YOUR SANDWICH

JUST ABOUT

I HOPE YOU SAVED SOME OF THE CRUSTS FOR THE BIRDS...

OF COURSE!

MERRY CHRISTMAS

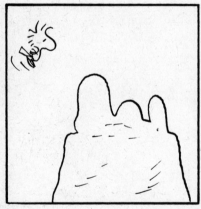

PEANUTS comic strips to follow: © 1978 United Feature Syndicate, Inc.

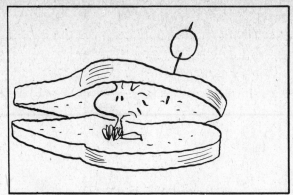

I'LL CLEAR THE TABLE, AND YOU STACK THE DISHES...

SAVE THOSE BREAD CRUMBS, LUCY...

THERE ARE BIRDS OUTSIDE WHO NEED THEM...

I NEVER THOUGHT OF THAT

BIRDS HAVE A HARD TIME FINDING FOOD WHEN THE GROUND IS COVERED WITH SNOW...

THERE, HOW WAS THAT?

I THINK YOU COULD HAVE SCATTERED THEM AROUND A LITTLE MORE...

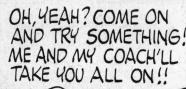

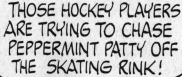

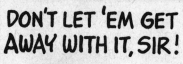

I DON'T EVEN REMEMBER WHAT HAPPENED, SIR...

WELL, THOSE HOCKEY PLAYERS WERE ABOUT TO GIVE ME A ROUGH TIME, AND YOU CAME RUNNING OUT TO HELP ME, MARCIE

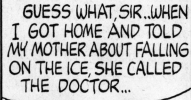

BUT I SLIPPED AND FELL ON THE ICE, HUH? I'LL SAY YOU DID!

LET'S GO BACK AND SHORTEN A FEW LIFE SPANS, SIR! LATER, MARCIE, LATER

GUESS WHAT, SIR..WHEN I GOT HOME AND TOLD MY MOTHER ABOUT FALLING ON THE ICE, SHE CALLED THE DOCTOR...

HE TOLD YOU TO TAKE IT EASY, HUH? WELL, THAT MAKES SENSE..CAN I GET YOU ANYTHING?

NO, THANK YOU, SIR... I'M JUST GOING TO LIE HERE, AND TRY TO READ "PILGRIM'S PROGRESS"

IF THE FALL ON THE ICE DIDN'T GIVE YOU A CONCUSSION, MARCIE, THAT WILL!

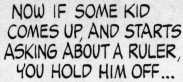